MY DOG, ME

MY DOG, ME

Rosemarie Perry

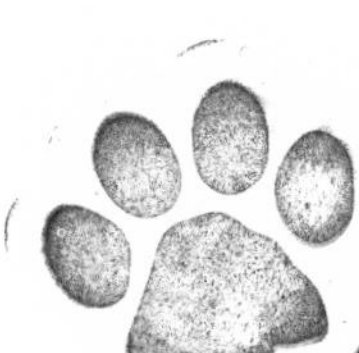

Woof!

ROSEMARIE PERRY
Illustrations by Heather Lowrie

ISBN-13: 9781535291491
ISBN-10: 1535291494

For my son, Tyler.

With special thanks to Mary Clark, Margo Bailey, April Lenar, and all my friends who encouraged me to complete this project.

CONTENTS

Chapter 1

AN ORDINARY DAY, ALMOST

Tyler heard the raindrops splashing against the bedroom window which was opened just a crack. He peeked through sleepy eyes to a gray sky. Tyler had no idea this would be his last ordinary day.

"Tyler, wake up," called Mom from the bottom of the staircase.

"OK, Mom," Tyler replied. "Oh, no, not morning already," said Tyler in a whisper. He yawned and stretched his arms into the air coming to rest on the furry head of his best friend, Dundee, an Australian shepherd dog from the humane society. "It's so gloomy. Even the sun is still under the covers. I sure wish I could stay home today like you, Dundee."

Dundee, a big blue eyed mess with black, brown, and white fur, nuzzled closer to his master, seeming to enjoy their mutual warmth.

"You're so lucky to be a dog," Tyler said without making a move toward getting out of bed. He rolled over toward his friend and continued, "You don't have to go to school or worry about homework or wonder if that pain, Alfred, is going to pull another nasty trick." After a long yawn he said, "It would be great not to have to stay away from Jessica. You know her. She's the one who told everyone she is going to kiss me before the end of the year."

Tyler heaved himself off the bed. "Dogs don't have to do chores. You don't even have to make the bed you sleep in." He shoved the dog toward the side of the bed. "Get off the bed, silly pooch, so I can smooth the covers. Just because you sleep in it doesn't mean you own it."

"Tyler, hurry!" said Mom from the bottom of the stairs. "You'll miss the bus. It's already quarter past seven."

"Yuppers, Mom," Tyler replied, grabbing clothes to wear. In a few minutes he yelled, "On my way," through a mouth full of toothpaste foam, his wavy light brown hair falling into his hazel eyes.

After gulping a glass of milk, Tyler grabbed a piece of toast with hazelnut spread, kissed his mom and said, "Later, Mom." He sprinted to the bus stop munching. Dundee was ahead of him with his tongue hanging out, no doubt looking forward to the loving pats of the other children and at least one leftover bite of toast from Tyler.

Three other students boarded the bus ahead of Tyler. "See you after school, buddy," Tyler yelled over his shoulder as the bus driver closed the door. Dundee sat and watched until the school bus groaned up the hill.

It was a pretty boring day at school. Alfred was absent. Tyler was relieved that Jessica seemed more interested in solving her math word problems than making a plan to kiss him. The whole day, it rained, and rained, and rained. Even Mrs. Duncan stifled a yawn from time to time.

By the end of the school day there were lots of deep puddles, great for jumping into but impossible to dodge when running the bases. It was drizzling as he boarded the school bus, a sure sign that baseball practice would be cancelled.

At 3:34 p.m. sharp, the yellow school bus slowed at the top of the hill near home. Dundee was already at the stop, his tail wagging in anticipation of seeing his master again.

"Hey there, pal," Tyler said as he descended the steps of the school bus. He scratched behind the dog's ears. In a flash, Dundee was standing on his hind legs, almost as tall as Tyler. "Get down with those wet paws," Tyler scolded. "You're the only dog I ever met who always wants to dance, even in the rain."

Normally, the other kids would take turns "dancing" with Dundee as they called, "Me next, Dundee. Dance with me." All the kids loved the dog and his sloshy welcome home kisses. Today, though, they ran through the raindrops to their homes, leaving Tyler the only one with muddy paw prints on his jacket.

Dark clouds rumbled throughout the evening. After dinner Tyler wrote his spelling words and took a shower. Just as he settled into bed with the latest superheroes book, Dundee, his favorite foot warmer, hopped on top of the striped comforter. When it seemed they were both settled and cozy, Dundee started to whine and jumped off the bed. Using his long snout, he nudged the bedroom door attempting to open it.

"What do you want, silly pest? To go out?"

Dundee just cocked his head and pawed at the door.

"You already went out," said an annoyed Tyler peering over his book.

That didn't satisfy the pup who continued to moan until Tyler got out of bed and opened the door. Dundee sprinted off and the sleepy boy grumbled as he followed him to the kitchen. Dundee came to a halt at the refrigerator and sat with a big doggie grin as his furry tail tapped on the floor.

"Oh, you want a meatball from dinner." Tyler took a big one from the plastic container and handed it to Dundee. "Here, you pest." It was gone in one swallow.

They returned to the bedroom, but before Tyler slipped under the covers, he noticed the lightening flashing in the distance. It gave the night sky an eerie green glow. The window was slightly open, as usual, and he couldn't remember it ever raining in. He patted the bed. Dundee, who was sitting on the floor nearby, jumped onto the covers next to Tyler.

Tyler noticed a pungent aroma like bleach but got distracted by his best friend circling around and around until he found his favorite spot. For a while they both watched the light show and listened to the rolling sounds of thunder. Tyler said, "Wouldn't it be fun if we could trade places for a day? I wish we could. It would be such fun, don't you think?

Tyler wondered what it would be like to spend the day as a dog. Dundee nudged his head under Tyler's soft warm hand. As they settled in for the night, Dundee leaned up and gave his forever friend a sloshy good night kiss. Too tired to pay any more attention to a funny smell in the air, Tyler adjusted his pillow and drifted to sleep under the comforter the same red and blue as his baseball uniform.

Chapter 2

SWITCHED

"Tyler, wake up," shouted a cheerful mom from downstairs. "It's 7:15. Hurry, or you'll miss the bus."

The sleepy boy, still snuggling under the covers, rubbed his hand along his cheek. He yawned and then crawled over to his furry friend. He sat on his heels and cocked his head from side to side before he reached over to pet the dog. But first the boy leaned forward, took a sniff and asked, "Who are you?" Then with a flash of recognition, the boy licked the dog's snout.

The kiss awakened the dog, who hopped off the bed and found his nose at the same level as the bed sheets. He attempted to stand on his back legs, but in a few seconds fell forward and found himself staring again at the edge of the bed. *What is happening? A strange dream, maybe.*

They both ran to the bathroom and stopped short in front of the full length mirror at the end of the hallway. They stood there shocked, staring at their reflections. The dog leaned closer and touched the mirror with a paw. *What happened? Oh my gosh… this can't be.*

His heart was beating so hard it might have burst out of his chest. He was panting and his tongue was hanging out of his mouth, like a dog. But… he was … a dog! Overnight Tyler had turned into a dog that looked just like Dundee!

Terrified, his eyes grew round as marbles as he started to cry out, "Mom, Mom." But the sounds came out in a big howl, "Owwww, Owwww," Tyler looked at himself again and thought, *OK, don't panic. I'm just a boy but I look like a dog. I act like a dog. I talk like a dog. Oh, no...*

"What's going on up there?" Mom questioned. "Hurry, son, your breakfast is getting cold."

To Tyler the world looked strange, all the colors were so dull and muted so that he couldn't clearly tell one from the other. The familiar aromas of Mom's coffee and her toast with butter calmed him. His panic subsided as he adjusted to this new situation. Tyler sprawled on the cool tile floor and put his paws on his snout looking up at Dundee, who was now human.

"Coming, Mom," replied Dundee as he flexed his human arms and smoothed his hair back with his hands. "Guess our wishes came true, huh, Tyler?"

Dundee noticed a finger that was away from the other four. "What's this for?" he asked Tyler as he wiggled it in the dog's face. "Oh, never mind," he said with a chuckle. "You can't talk. Guess I'll have to figure that out."

Dundee splashed water on his face. Then he stared at the battery operated toothbrush. "Hmm, no time to figure this out."

He went back to his bedroom and saw the clothes that mom had picked out for Tyler, an orange polo shirt and blue jeans hanging over the chair to his desk. Dundee stopped. He stared at them and then looked around his room.

"Wow, the world looks different." He rubbed his eyes and said, "I never knew there are so many colors!" Dundee turned around in awe and noticed the red and blue striped comforter on the bed, running his fingers along the lines of colors. When he opened the closet, he stood in awe of clothing in so many colors, it made him squint.

Looking out the window, Dundee gazed at the shiny green leaves swaying on the trees and a blue jay sitting on a branch. Two gray squirrels were chasing each other. He noticed the brown and green print of the camo on his backpack.

He ran to the mirror over the dresser and peered into a reflection with eyes the same green as the camo in his backpack but peppered with specks of gold. There was a sprinkle of little brown smudges covering his nose and little indentions on his cheeks. So many differences in this human body made him shudder. He ran his hands over his arms – no fur. "This feels weird," he said to Tyler. The palms of his hands were moist with sweat and his heart was pounding as he brushed the hair from his forehead.

"Son, ten minutes till the bus," said Mom, the pitch of her voice rising.

Dundee struggled into the pants automatically using his "new" finger. "Oh, so this finger helps you grab and hold things. OK!" Calmer now, he pulled on the shirt and canvas sneakers, then began sniffing for the backpack but got nothing in the way he usually found things.

"What's wrong with my nose?" He began to panic realizing he no longer had his superior sense of smell. But with his vision more prominent, he noticed the backpack in the corner and slung it over his shoulder. With his heartbeat finally subsiding, a calmer Dundee said to his master lying nearby, "Tyler, wow, I get to go to school for you today, just like we wanted. Yippee… I think!"

No, woofed Tyler.

"You always said I'm a smart dog. I'll copy what the other kids do. It will be fun," replied Dundee, gaining confidence in this new wonderful body.

He felt the need to relieve himself and laughed when he got to the toilet and had to lean against the wall because his one leg kept lifting. "Weird," he said as he adjusted his pants.

"Tyler, I hear the bus," warned Mom.

"OK, Mom. I can't wait to go to school today," said Dundee stifling a smile. He covered his mouth with one hand, since his tongue kept wanting to hang out of it, and scurried down the stairs.

"What's up, little man? All I heard yesterday is that you wish you could be a dog and stay home from school for a change," Mom said.

"Today's special," Dundee said turning to Tyler who started to whine. "Gotta go, buddy. Be a good dog, today." Dundee slipped a big bite of toast to Tyler. Then he gave Mom a quick kiss saying, "Love you, Mom," and hurried out the door to the bus stop, running on two legs instead of his usual four. It took longer this way, especially carrying a heavy backpack.

Tyler didn't go with him. Instead, the dog sat on the top of the couch near the big window and stared at the boy running toward the other students. He rested his head on a cushion and covered his snout with his paws.

Mom sat on the couch watching to make sure all the students got on the bus. She patted the family dog on the head and said into his blue eyes, “What’s the matter, Dundee? You look like a sad doggie today. Tyler will be home before you know it.” She kissed his snout and said with a smile, “Come on. You need to go out. When you come back, I’ve got a deer chew stick for you, your favorite.”

Oh, great, just what I want to chew on. Bleah. Then the urge overcame him, and Tyler nosed past the screen door to “water” Dundee’s favorite bush in the backyard.

Chapter 3

THE BIG LIE

Dundee sat by himself on the bus and gazed out the window. *I'm scared. I don't know what to do. I'm just a dog. What if they find out? What will happen to me?*

But before Dundee could worry any longer, the bus creaked to a stop at the door of the school. The other children stood in line to get off, then ran into the building.

Where should I go? thought Dundee as he entered the front door of the school. Rushing past him, Tyler's best friend, Kevin said, "Race you to Mrs. Duncan's room." In a flash Kevin blended in among the other children in the hallway.

Dundee followed him with difficulty running on two legs instead of four. And his book bag kept falling off his shoulder. After a warning from a tall lady with big red glasses to slow down, *probably the top dog around here,* Kevin and Dundee stopped at Room 221.

Dundee saw the petite brown haired lady in the blue sweater standing at the door. Small round glasses hung on a silver chain around her neck. The teacher greeted her students as they entered her classroom.

She must be Mrs. Duncan. I recognize her voice.

"Good morning, boys," said a cheery voice.

"Good morning, Mrs. Duncan," replied a sing-song Dundee and Kevin.

As they hung up their book bags, Kevin asked, "Hey, Tyler, did you study for the spelling test?"

"No, I forgot," stuttered Dundee. *Oh, this is swell. I can't spell a thing. I can't even hold a pencil. What'll I do now?* He slid into the seat next to Kevin.

"Tyler, what are you doing?" asked Kevin. That's Jessica's seat. She's gonna come in any minute and kiss you right here in front of everybody. Quick, get to your own seat."

Dundee bolted up and looked around. *But where is my seat?* There were lots of desk in neat rows. *Which one is Tyler's?* He stopped to think for a minute. *Ha,* he laughed. *Of course. How silly of me not to think of this earlier.*

The other students stopped and stared as Dundee started sniffing all the desks in the classroom. He sure looked funny with his nose pressed to the tops of the desks, the seats, and the papers. *Darn, I can't smell like I used to when I was a dog.*

Dundee didn't notice but all the other students and Mrs. Duncan just stared at him for a minute. Some of the kids shrugged their shoulders, some laughed. Mrs. Duncan just shook her head and smiled.

Kevin pointed to a desk and said, “There, you dodo bird. Did you forget your glasses?”

Dundee quickly turned in a circle and sat down, proud of his quick thinking. *Wow, this is great. I really can do this. No one will ever know I’m a dog. But I really do miss my nose.* Dundee stifled a chuckle as he folded his hands on the desk and smiled at Mrs. Duncan. *I can figure things out for myself. Neat.*

After the Pledge of Allegiance, which Dundee managed by mouthing the words, Mrs. Duncan said, “Boys and girls, it’s time for your spelling test. Get out a sheet of paper and number from one to ten.”

Dundee fumbled with the paper and the pencil using two hands, but that was as far as he got. *I don’t know how to write or how to spell. Shucks, I don’t even know how to hold a pencil.* He rested his chin in his hand, an elbow propped up on the desk.

Mrs. Duncan noticed. “What’s the matter, Tyler?”

Dundee lifted his eyes to his teacher and didn’t move.

Kevin piped in. “He probably didn’t study his spelling, Mrs. Duncan.”

“Well,” the teacher replied. “See how many you can spell, anyway. Trust yourself. See the words in your head and write them down. You might surprise yourself.”

Dundee clumsily picked up his pencil as Mrs. Duncan began calling out the words. He tried to remember how to spell. Forming the letters was difficult.

Mrs. Duncan noticed Dundee’s frustration. As she gathered the students’ papers, she paused by him and said, “What’s wrong today, Tyler? You seem out of sorts.”

Out of sorts! You call this out of sorts? Dundee felt like howling but just shrugged his shoulders. “I had a rough night, Mrs. Duncan, with the storm and all.”

“Maybe you’ll feel better after recess,” she said with a smile and a pat on his shoulder.

Recess, what is recess? We never have recess at home. Dundee tried to remember the meaning of that word. He looked around to see the other students putting their things in their desks and getting up to stand in a line. Reverting to his pack mentality, Dundee did the same, got into the line, and followed the other students onto the playground. The blacktop still had some wet places from last night’s storm, but the sun was shining. Some puddles looked like they were drying up.

“Come on, Tyler. Let’s toss the ball around,” yelled Kevin slinging a baseball from one hand to the other.

Oh, no, how do you catch a baseball? Dundee watched the players plenty of times but he never actually caught one, unless you count the foul ball he caught in his mouth when it rolled from first base.

Kevin threw the ball and Dundee just watched it fly by. He thought Kevin might get suspicious if he ran after it and picked it up with his mouth. And he didn't want to embarrass himself by not being able to catch it with his hands.

"Wake up, Tyler," Kevin said as he ran to get it. "How do you expect to make shortstop for the team, if you're day-dreaming instead of reaching for the ball?" He picked it up and said, "Dundee would be a better player than you. Maybe you should wear your glasses."

Kevin's scolding faded into the background as Dundee inhaled all the smells in the playground. From the corner of his eye, he noticed something running on the ground. *Squirrel!*

He remembered how much fun it was to chase those little critters and couldn't resist following the one that scurried right in front of him. Although he ran as fast as he could, the squirrel ran up the big oak tree at the edge of the playground.

Out of breath, Dundee thought, *So, maybe this is why humans never catch squirrels. Being a dog is lots more fun.* Dundee looked up at the squirrel sitting on a branch, flicking his tail,. "Oh, so you think this is funny. Lucky for you I'm on two legs today or I'd bring you as a surprise to Mrs. Duncan," he said.

Kevin ran over to Dundee who was ignoring the bell ending recess. He overheard Dundee talking to the squirrel. He grabbed his friend's arm and said shaking his head, "Come on, Tyler. The bell rang minutes ago. What are you doing over here at the far edge of the playground? Hurry, we'll be late to class."

Dundee looked over his shoulder and gave that squirrel a look that said, "Wait till tomorrow."

Kevin said, "What do you mean, 'Lucky for you I'm on two legs today'?"

"Oh, yeah," Dundee replied. "I mean that squirrel sure is lucky I'm not a dog, or he'd be a gonner by now."

"Dundee would have caught that squirrel for sure," said Kevin chuckling.

"Right," said Dundee nodding his head. "I'm … uh, Dundee is a really smart dog."

Chapter 4

MORE LIES

After recess, Mrs. Duncan called the students to line up at the water fountain. Alfred got to the head of the line and waved his hand for Dundee to get behind him. Alfred pressed the button and slurped water that tumbled like a small waterfall into the basin. When no one was looking, he cupped his hand under the water, then turned and threw it at Dundee saying, “Don’t bother to drink it. You already got some.” Alfred started giggling, then scampered off to the classroom.

Dundee muttered under his breath, “I could just bite that kid.” Droplets of water stained his shirt. Trying to ignore Alfred, Dundee said, “Actually a cool drink sounds like a really good idea.” He stepped on the box in front of the fountain but couldn’t figure how to turn the water on.

“Hurry up, Tyler,” echoed several students who were in line.

Dundee looked at the silver faucet and the place where water drained. Since water was always provided for him in a bowl at home, he had no idea what to do. He stared and tried to figure it out. He wiggled the faucet and bumped the water fountain, looking longingly at the remaining droplets left by Alfred.

"Come on, Tyler," said Kevin. "What's the problem?"

In frustration, Dundee shoved the water fountain with his left hand. It landed on the silver button and out came a long, high spray of water. He tried to remember how to drink from a fountain since he had only seen Tyler drinking from a cup at home. He hit the button again but the water appeared for only a few seconds.

After several tries, he bent his head over and slurped the water as it swirled into the drain and disappeared.

As the boy straightened up, his face and hair were dripping. He shook his head from side to side, slinging water droplets all over the wall and the floor. Some of the girls were giggling. The boys looked confused. Everyone headed back to class.

Hmmmph, and after I licked the bowl clean too. He smiled. *No one suspects I'm a dog. I can even work the water fountain.* Nodding he thought, *I really am a smart dog.*

When he got back to his seat, the other students had their social studies books out and Mrs. Duncan was grading papers. Dundee flipped open his book to the section on Africa and looked at the photographs. He had never seen such creatures, only other dogs and the neighbor's cat who roamed the neighborhood. Although, in the backyard there were a few birds and some squirrels.

One animal in the book towered as high as some trees. It was light colored with irregular spots. *Interesting, skinny legs and what a long neck.* Another was big and fat with a tiny tail. *What a nose!* It curled under his body and could inhale water. *Amazing.* He wondered where these animals sleep and the kind of houses they live in and what they like to eat. He struggled to remember their names.

Kevin noticed and said, "Tyler, you're such an animal lover. We're supposed to be reading about the geography and farming in Africa, not going on safari with animals."

Tyler gave him a dirty look.

"OK, so you belong in a zoo, but I still think you're my best friend," Kevin said chuckling.

"Right," Tyler replied and tried to think of something clever to say to the head honcho of his pack of friends. But he was distracted by the most wonderful aroma. Food! He sniffed once, twice, then knew. *Hamburgers and French fries. Yippee!* He didn't hear one word that Mrs. Duncan said all through the rest of social studies. He just sat with his tongue hanging out of his mouth and a silly grin on his face.

Dundee's eyes drifted toward Jessica. She was giggling. *Great, just great. I probably look silly.* He covered his mouth with his hand and looked away, embarrassed.

As Mrs. Duncan announced, "Lunchtime," Dundee ran to the front of the line, but then he felt a panic as his eyes darted from side to side. *Gosh, I've never eaten lunch in school. I don't know what to do. Tyler always breaks off a bite for me.* Dundee slinked back through the line just behind Kevin. *I'll just do what he does. Boy that food sure smells great. Yum! Food, food, food!*

In the cafeteria Dundee slid his tray along a rail, just like Kevin. The nice lunch ladies gave each student a hamburger, some French fries, carrot sticks, a sugar cookie, an apple, and a carton of milk. He was so excited his hands were shaking. The tray landed on the table with a bang, and Dundee plopped down and leaned over his food.

He stopped and looked around. The other students picked up the food using that little finger set away from the other fingers. *Wow, nice paws, these humans have.*

But before he could figure how to hold the hamburger or pick up a French fry, Dundee couldn't help himself. He dived into his tray head first, devoured the hamburger in three bites and wolfed down the fries. He inhaled the cookie and looked around. The other kids at the lunch table were staring at him. He smiled and said, "I'm starving. Aren't you?"

"You sure are, Tyler," said Kevin laughing. "Are you learning manners from Dundee?" The other kids laughed in agreement and continued eating.

Dundee passed on the apple and carrots because he couldn't figure out how to hold them. Embarrassed, he had to stop himself from licking the tray clean. *Lucky that Mrs. Duncan is sitting at the teachers' table and doesn't notice.*

After lunch the class was ready for DEAR Time – Drop Everything and Read. Dundee was so glad to rest.

The students went to their favorite reading spots. A few stayed in their seats while others opted to sit on a pillow and lean against the bookshelf. Dundee recognized Tyler's beanbag chair located in a cozy spot near the window. He turned around three times before finally settling in with a book about birds. Being a human was really exhausting, even for a smart dog. The sunlight was warm and it wasn't long before he leaned on his side. "I'm so tired," he said softly to no one in particular.

He noticed Jessica only pretended to read as she flipped the pages of her book, her eyes straying from the book to his direction. He overheard her whisper to her friend, a girl with pigtails and braces, "He is so cute."

Dundee turned over to look at Kevin who not reading either. He lay on his back with his hands behind his head, maybe thinking about the cheers when he hit a grand slam homer.

In a few moments Dundee's eyes were heavy with sleep. He turned on his side and made gestures like a dog running, but no one noticed. He was dreaming about catching that silly squirrel and bringing it to surprise Mrs. Duncan.

Chapter 5

THE SCIENCE LESSON

"Silent reading time is up, my darlings," said Mrs. Duncan as she rang a little bell on her desk. "When you get back to your seats, we'll have today's science lesson – Color." The students reluctantly put their books away and returned to their desks.

On each desk were a handful of paint chip samples from the hardware store. She continued, "You can see that we can make paint in hundreds of colors. Each one is blended from mixing primary colors along with adding white or black."

Dundee thought about what his teacher said. *I saw Mom paint Tyler's room once. Not sure I want to paint our classroom. Think I'll just let the other students do it.* But when everyone else seemed excited, Dundee joined the others in the pack, not wanting to miss anything.

She went on to ask the class to name the primary colors. "Yes, the primary colors are red, blue, and yellow."

He noticed that while the students had been busy reading, Mrs. Duncan and her teacher aide, roly poly Mrs. Archer, had set up the easels in the back of the classroom.

"Today each of you will have the opportunity to create colors," said Mrs. Duncan in an excited voice.

"Cool," said Kevin, his excitement echoed by the other students.

Mrs. Duncan continued, "Each of you will have three pots of finger paint: two primary colors and white or black. You are to blend your two colors with the third to create a new color. Don't be afraid to experiment. If you are careful, you can share your paints with the student next to you. Tomorrow we'll talk about your results and how we get a variety of colors from the three primary ones."

The students put on their painting shirts. With a small bowl of water and three pots of finger paints in the center of the easel tray, they were ready to paint on the shiny white paper.

Mrs. Duncan started playing a CD of Mozart. "Mozart started composing beautiful music when he was a little guy. Let's see what colors you create. We'll talk about your discoveries tomorrow after your paintings dry. Any questions?"

"Wow, this is so fun," said Kevin. He turned to Dundee and whispered, "If we play our cards right, we can run over into math time." Kevin put blue and yellow paint on the paper. Then he added a dot of black. "Look," Kevin said. "I made green like my turtle."

Dundee stared at the colors that Kevin was mixing, still as a statue.

Mrs. Duncan came over to Dundee. "Tyler, you haven't begun yet. Just go ahead and start painting. I bet there's a masterpiece waiting to form on the paper."

"Yes, Ma'm," Dundee replied. He turned back to the paints. Slowly, he touched one. It was sticky and had a funny smell. He leaned closer to sneak a few sniffs when no one was looking. He almost took a lick, but figured everyone would notice his stained tongue or a blotch of paint around his mouth and under his nose. Touching the paper, he enjoyed the feeling of the paint as he made circles on the paper. Circles – a new movement for him. When he was a dog, he never moved his paws in a circle.

Kevin was laughing and flicking the paints to form splotches on the paper. Dundee turned his head to look at Jessica, who was nearby. She had two colors that she was mixing. First she mixed red with yellow, then added some white. She made wavy horizontal stripes on her paper. She turned to Dundee and said, "Tyler, look. I made a sunrise."

"It's bea – u- ti- ful," said Dundee with his mouth slightly open in awe.

"May I have some of your blue?" she asked leaning over to his color pots.

Dundee nodded but all he could say over and over again was, "Wow."

Jessica dipped her pinkie finger into his blue, then added a bit of it to her red. With a touch of white she created the most wonderful blue-purple color. She spread some at the top of her paper. "Look, Tyler. It's the sky while the sun is still snoozing."

Dundee realized that humans not only see the world in multiple hues, but can actually create colors. "Wow," he said over and over again as he walked around to observe the masterpieces nearby, lost in a kaleidoscope of colors.

Kevin said, "Tyler, you'd better hurry and blend your colors. Some kids are already finished."

His memory of the canine view of the world in shades of gray seemed very far away.

Mrs. Duncan put her hand on his shoulder gently. "Tyler, it's time to clean up. Didn't you hear me? You must be enjoying this lesson about color." Dundee nudged his head under her hand and Mrs. Duncan gave him a pat on the head. It felt so good. *Humans are easy to train,* he decided.

As he cleared his desk, he realized the shift taking place as his eyes completely overpowered his sense of smell, which had dominated his life as a dog. He stood still and looked around at the other students. *I can learn. I want to understand why humans see colors and dogs don't. And, how humans make books and music. I love school.* He made a decision. *How can I break it to Tyler that I want to stay a human?*

Mrs. Duncan interrupted Dundee's thoughts when she clapped her hands. "Let's all go to the restroom and wash our hands."

Dundee looked up. *Restroom? What's a restroom? I thought we already rested.* He looked for his friend who was already at the head of the line. *Guess I'll have to watch Kevin again. He would have been a great top dog.* Dundee smiled and got into line.

Chapter 6

AFTERNOON CLASSES

The boys and girls lined up on opposite sides of the hallway. The boys went into one room and the girls went into the other one. Dundee thought it was silly to call this a restroom since there were no couches, just a row of funny looking white ceramic objects attached to the wall. *What are those white things for? We don't have any at home.* There were a few toilets near the back wall. Dundee lagged behind the other boys and watched Kevin.

"Hey, Tyler, what are you looking at?" asked Kevin who relieved himself.

"Nothing." Dundee felt awkward. He had seen Tyler go to the bathroom before and he did his best this morning at home. But hurrying, he struggled with the zipper in his pants as he tried to imitate the other boys at the ceramic basin.

The worst part was that his leg kept wanting to lift and he wobbled on one leg. Giving up, Dundee used his hands against the wall to keep from falling over. *It's a lot harder trying to balance on one leg than on three legs. Guess I need more practice.* His face turned red in frustration.

"What a weirdo," said Alfred, who noticed Dundee teetering.

Kevin thought it was funny and started to laugh. So did the other boys.

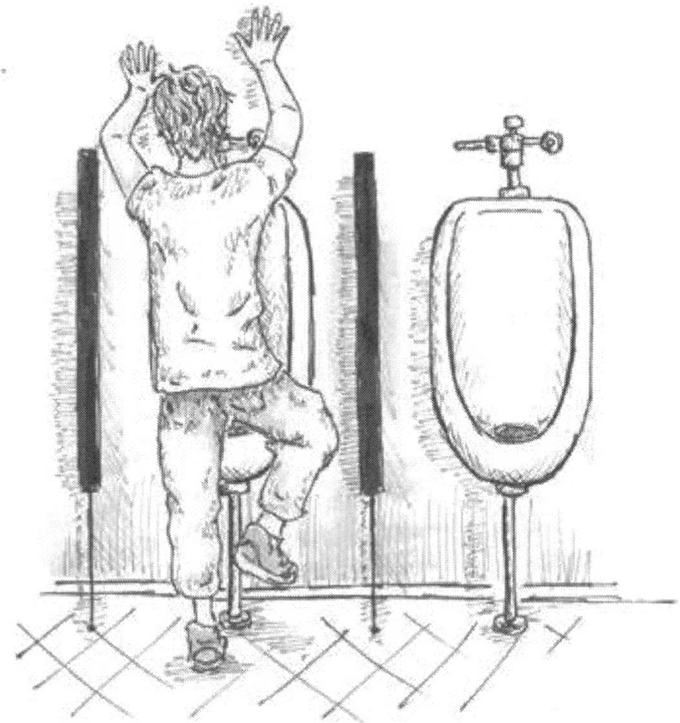

Mrs. Duncan called into the restroom. "What's so funny in there? Come on, boys."

The others splashed water onto each other as they washed their hands, and then scurried back to the line.

Dundee hurried outside without stopping at the sink. Stifled giggles greeted him. He pretended to ignore the other boys.

When they entered the classroom Mrs. Duncan said, "Math time" as she passed out papers.

Oh, great, Math. Dundee passed the math worksheets behind him to Jessica. He felt a knot in his stomach when he saw the assignment. He felt like crying because all the signs and symbols looked strange to him. He put his fist to his mouth. *I don't understand this.*

"Let's practice what we learned yesterday," said Mrs. Duncan brightly.

Dundee looked around. Kevin and Alfred were bent over their worksheets. Jessica was erasing. He still couldn't figure how to hold a pencil so he could pretend to work the problems.

I love school but I can't do this anymore. All this thinking is too hard and I'm exhausted trying so hard to fit in with the other students. "I want to go home," Dundee cried softly changing his mind about staying a boy.

Mrs. Duncan was preparing a lesson at her desk and didn't notice Dundee's frustration. Jessica did. She came over to him and said, "I'll help you, Tyler. I know that math is hard for you. We'll do it together."

Just then, Dundee was overwhelmed with gratitude. *She's so pretty and so nice. She smells like apples.* In that moment Dundee forgot himself, leaned over and gave her a great big wet doggie kiss on the cheek.

"Ouuuuu," shrieked Jessica. "I'll never want to kiss a boy as long as I live!" She wiped her shirt sleeve over her shining cheek. "And, you can do your math yourself!" she pouted as she went back to her seat.

The class giggled. Mrs. Duncan was so absorbed in her work that when she glanced up Jessica had already sat down.

Dundee felt awful. He didn't mean to upset Jessica and was embarrassed. He began to daydream. *I wonder what Tyler is doing at home.*

He looked out the window. It had started to rain.

Chapter 7

A DOG'S LIFE

A *deer chew stick?* Tyler whined at Mom who was still drinking her morning coffee. *You really expect me to eat this? Do you know who I am?* But then Mom swiped the treat under Tyler's nose and without any further thought, he jumped up and crunched it like a hungry dinosaur. It was gone in two bites. Tyler licked his lips. *Not bad, not bad at all. Tastes like chicken.*

Mom was getting ready to go to work. She shooed Tyler out the back door. "Do your business, Dundee," she said.

Business? Then an urge overcame Tyler and he ran for the fire hydrant. Without thinking he lifted his leg and a yellow stream dripped over it, puddling at the bottom. *OK!*

Tyler almost gasped at all the smells that overcame him. *Oh, yeah, a dog's sense of smell is way better than humans. Whoa...* Tyler sniffed the air. From the front yard he could recognize all the smells of each child who had waited by the hydrant for the bus stop: Claire's peanut butter sandwich for lunch, Sean's gym shoes, and a wrapper containing a piece of Conor's breakfast biscuit of sausage and eggs. *That kid never picks up anything.* He could smell the candy that had been in the empty wrapper on the street and the mint growing in the planter. *Oops, a wad of bubble gum. Yuck. Better jump over that.* And then the smell of, of, of rabbits!

He hopped over the holly bushes, hoping to scare the rabbits out of their hiding place. After a few barks and some scratching at the dirt, he gave up. *Darn. Guess nobody's home. Oh, well.*

Tyler spied the neighbor's gray tabby cat hiding behind the big oak tree, crouched low on all fours, stalking some robins looking for worms. *Oh, no you don't.* Tyler, baring his teeth and growling, had the feline dashing away as if Dundee were some cat eating monster. *Huh, what do you know?*

With his legs moving like a locomotive, he raced from one smell to another. *Guess four legs are better than two for running. Dogs would make great center fielders. Too bad they can't catch.* He heard the sound of the wind in his floppy ears. Tyler kicked up his heels in excitement and enjoying sprinting around trees and dodging plants, running, just to be running, until he spied the chipmunks.

Screeching to a halt and with his head bent low, he peered at one, and then the other. He couldn't tell which was Chip and which was Dale. That's what Mom always called them. One look at Tyler and they scurried over each other to their hole in the ground. *Scaredy cats.*

After chasing the neighbor's gray tabby cat up a tree, Tyler ran back to the yard enjoying the crackling of long fallen leaves rustling at his paws. He lifted his nose and continued smelling all the aromas of the morning, like coffee.

"Dundee," called Mom from the porch, holding her favorite cup. "Hey, wild thing, come back here. Some people in this house have to go to work."

Because he was a good dog, Tyler rushed back to Mom who gave him a kiss on the snout and ruffled his ears. Then Mom lifted her purse and car keys from the kitchen counter. After saying, "Be a good dog, Dundee," she left for work.

Why does Mom say that every time? She already knows I'm a good dog. Tyler stretched on the carpet by the door before lying down. *Humans...*

Chapter 8

A LONG DOGGIE DAY

Looking out the long window by the front door, Tyler watched Mom pull out of the driveway and go up the hill, just like the school bus. He finished his kibble breakfast. *Not bad when you get used to it.* Then he drank some water.

Afterwards he scampered upstairs and looked around. He sniffed at the clothes on the floor and found a half-eaten granola bar in a shirt pocket, then followed his nose around the rest of the house. Gobbled up a small piece of popcorn that was wedged between the cushions of the couch. He thought about watching TV, but couldn't press the buttons on the remote. Trying to read was even more difficult since it was impossible to turn the pages. Even licking his paws didn't help. *Who knew I would miss my thumbs so much?*

Tyler found a napping spot near the garden window where the sun warmed the carpet. *Hey, this isn't so bad. I don't have to make my bed and I won't have any homework to do. Yippee!* He settled his head on his front paws. Then he raised his head. *Wait a minute,* he thought, *being a dog for a day might be OK, but what if I stay a dog forever?* He yawned and stretched his front paws. *I'll think about that after my nap.* The warm sunlight brushed away his fears and he fell asleep.

It was a peacock, a big beautiful squawking bird, its feathers displayed like a fan with beady eyes running to attack Tyler. But the "good" dog was ready to pounce, his head ducked low and growling.

"Brrrinnnggg, Brrrinnngg."

Huh? What? Tyler lifted his head and opened his eyes. He was back in his spot, breathing heavily. Lifting up onto his front paws, he shook his head. *Just a dream.*

"Brrrinnnggg."

Oh, the phone. Tyler set his head down and brushed his snout with his paws. He rolled over onto his side and drifted off as the caller left a message on the answering machine.

A short time later, the doorbell rang. Without thinking, Tyler jumped up and began to bark. He looked out the window. It was the UPS driver leaving a package on the front porch for Mom. *Geez.* He returned to his spot and lay on his back, paws up. But he couldn't sleep. Nothing to see on the ceiling. *This is boring.*

Then Tyler went into the kitchen and lapped some water from his bowl. He saw the rug near the fireplace. It was on the opposite side of the house next to the den. *Looks comfy.* He trotted over and settled down.

A loud buzz from outside woke Tyler. At first he thought it was part of a dream, but the sound droned on and on. *What the heck is that noise?* By now Tyler was irritated. He propped his paws on the window sill and tried to look between the blinds. It was Tony, the retired next door neighbor, cutting his lawn.

From there Tyler went to check his bowl, in case by magic some doggie snacks might appear. But it was empty. He licked the dry bowl and trotted back to the front window. He looked up and down the street. All was quiet. *Great.* The canine snuggled up next to the couch away from the window and the sunshine. It was a nice, quiet, dark spot. He curled up into a ball near Mom's favorite chair. He snoozed with her scent nearby.

"Bam. Bang. Clang." Tyler bolted upright. The loud noise scared him and he was shivering. He shook his head and went to the window.

It was the city garbage truck emptying the bins left near the street.

Now, I know why dogs go after the men who pick up garbage. They are the worst for interrupting nap time. Grrrr.

Tyler sighed and decided to go upstairs. *Hmmm, maybe I should slide under the bed? Why didn't I think of this before? OK, maybe I'm not such a smart dog.* Something made him pause as he struggled to push himself through the narrow space under the bed. He heard a familiar car sound, a door slam, and footsteps on the back porch.

He knew who it was. She smelled like lilies of the valley. He hopped down the stairs and rubbed his whole body against her leg.

"Hello, my darling," Mom said. She leaned down and took his head between her hands. Her hazel eyes were sparkling and she had a big smile on her face. After a long scratch behind his ears, Mom bent over and kissed his snout. Tyler was so happy to see her. "Did you have a nice doggie day?"

Tyler whined. *I hope your day wasn't as frustrating as mine.*

"Come on. Let's go out for a while," she said while attaching his leash.

Yes, a walk, outside! Tyler could hardly stand still his tail was wagging so hard.

After she put on a sweater and got the leash, they walked down the stairs and started around the block. It had been a long time since he and Mom had gone for a walk together, just the two of them. Mom chatted about what was on her mind, what she might make for dinner, about the upcoming PTA meeting, baseball practice. It really didn't matter. It was just wonderful to listen to her voice and walk alongside her. Tyler felt very close to his mom. *I wonder if she has any idea…*

They stopped to let two college kids on bicycles pass. Tyler licked mom's hand. She leaned over and patted his head. "I do so love you, Dundee. You know, I loved you first, before Tyler was born. You're my favorite friend in the whole world."

A neighbor who was outside digging weeds stood up when she saw them coming. The two women started chatting.

Wait a minute. Tyler just stood still for a minute, his head cocked one way, then the other. *I thought I was your favorite, not Dundee. I'm your son.* Then he remembered, *She doesn't know.*

After a few seconds, he thought, *I don't care. I won't be second, not even to Dundee.* Feeling jealous, a plan began to form in Tyler's brain. *I may just have to get into some doggie trouble. Then she'll change her mind about who she loves more.*

Chapter 9

THE PLOT THICKENS

Tyler took off in a gallop, leaving the leash flapping in the wind behind him. He ran across the neighbor's yard to the main street. Without thinking he dashed into the traffic causing cars to swerve out of the way.

Mom came running after him. "Dundee, come here, you bad dog," she shouted. "Dundee, come."

The dog came barreling towards Mom trampling the neighbor's freshly planted petunias. Upon reaching Mom, Tyler jumped up to his familiar "wanna dance" stance and left doggie paw prints on Mom's new white sweater. He stopped long enough for Mom to grab his leash. Then, Tyler took off, making Mom breathless from the pace.

At the front door, Mom caught her breath and she scolded, "Dundee, you wild thing." She frowned. "Bad dog. What has gotten into you today?" she asked. "No treats for bad doggies."

Darn. He stopped for a drink at his water bowl and looked up at Mom. *I'm starving. What I wouldn't give a piece of hotdog.*

Tyler couldn't decide whether to be proud for making Mom upset or angry at himself for missing his favorite treat. He figured it was worth it.

He scooted upstairs to his bedroom and jumped on the bed with his dirty paws, leaving a trail of dirt behind him. *This will really get to her – dirt on the bed.*

When Mom started to make dinner and didn't go upstairs, Tyler decided to knock over a lamp or two, just to get Mom's attention.

Crash! Down went the catcher's mitt lamp. Plunk! The baseball trophies tumbled from the nightstand.

That got Mom's attention. She came bolting upstairs and stopped at the doorway.

She would have made a pretty fair greyhound, Tyler thought with a smirk.

Mom shook her finger at the dog. "Dundee, that's enough. Get outside on the porch. I don't know what's gotten into you today." She put her hand holding the dishcloth on her hip. "I don't like you when you do these things."

Perfect. It's working. Dundee will not be number one in this house. Just wait till I'm back. She'll really appreciate me then.

A thought caused Tyler to sit still as ceramic dog. *What if I stay a dog forever? What if Mom is so mad at me that she takes me to the pound? Or if I lose my family?* He started to howl a horrible, mournful wailing sound that surprised even himself.

Mom grabbed him by the collar and ushered him onto the screened in porch. "You just stay out there, bad doggie. You did this to yourself. You know better." She turned around and headed for the kitchen without even a glance back at a very sorrowful canine.

Chapter 10

LATE AFTERNOON

Tyler stretched out and tried to figure a way out of his dilemma. He was distracted by the familiar groan of the school bus as it got louder and louder finally stopping on the corner. There was no doubt it was THE bus.

Using his nose he inched open the screen door and ran as fast as his four legs could carry him. He waited as one by one the children got off the bus, Kevin and Dundee being the last two. While Dundee was struggling with his backpack, Kevin bent over to greet Tyler.

Kevin scratched Tyler's chin and asked, "Wanna dance?"

But Tyler ignored Kevin. Instead he jumped onto Dundee and whined. They both hugged each other a long time.

"You guys are so weird," said Kevin as he headed for his house. There was the far off sound of thunder. "Look at the sky," he said looking back. "It's so gray. Maybe baseball practice will be cancelled again. See you tomorrow."

He never noticed that Tyler and Dundee sat on the corner and huddled together. Even as the wind picked up and the raindrops began, they sat there hugging each other.

It started to rain harder. "We'd better get home, buddy," Dundee said. He led the way as they shuffled towards home.

"Oh, Tyler," Dundee began. "I missed you so much. But being a human is wonderful! I love all the colors. Mrs.

Duncan is nice. Jessica is so pretty and kind. But she doesn't like kisses, so don't worry. She thinks they're yukky."

Tyler smiled, his tongue hanging out as they picked up the pace.

Dundee continued. "Cafeteria food is great! And there are more squirrels in the playground than I have ever seen around here. Although I couldn't figure how to hold a pencil, couldn't do math, and struggled at the water fountain, I don't think anyone suspected I'm not you."

Great, whined Tyler. *Well, actually, I kind of enjoyed being you for a day. You run so fast and everything smells so interesting. Guess that's what happens when your nose is so close to the ground.* He stopped to sniff an unseen something in the grass. When he pried himself away, he continued, *Mom really loves you.*

"I know," Dundee replied. "I can't wait to see her and give her a hug."

Gotta tell you, said Tyler, *I'm kind of jealous. Thought I was Number One with her. Maybe I'm Number One on two legs and you're Number One with four legs.*

"Sure."

And something else – doggie biscuits aren't so bad. Sleeping in the sunbeams shining through the window sure feels good. But…I think I want to be a boy again.

"Uh, oh," said Dundee under his breath.

Tyler continued walking, his tail wagging. *I miss not being able to read. I really do want to learn math. I might even let Jessica kiss me.*

"No worries there, friend," said Dundee as he rolled his eyes. "You know, Tyler, I loved going to school today. There are lots of neat smells there that we don't have at home and so many interesting things to do. I didn't understand them all. But what I loved best was the science lesson in creating colors using finger paints. Now that was really cool." His excitement continued. "And, you know" he said with a sly grin, I almost caught a squirrel for Mrs. Duncan."

No way. Tyler shook his head sideways and grinned a big doggie grin.

Then Dundee paused. "But it sure is tiring being a human. I'm exhausted. There are so many things to learn, like math. And what to do with Alfred."

Tyler nodded his head.

"It's really hard pretending to be you." Dundee adjusted his backpack. "Maybe, I do miss being a dog. Is it OK if I want to be a dog again?"

The two friends looked at each other, reading each other's minds. "What if that never happens?" said Dundee, his voice panicky.

What if you are stuck being a boy and I am a dog forever? Tyler moaned his dismay.

Dundee stared into the distance and patted Tyler on the head. The sky opened up and big sheets of rain drenched them both in a minute. "Quick, Tyler, let's run home."

Tyler and Dundee tried to run between the raindrops but their feet felt like lead. They trudged along with heavy hearts at the predicament in which they found themselves. By the time they reached home, both were soaking wet. It didn't matter. The two friends both were crying tears that blended with the raindrops on their faces.

Chapter 11

A BIG PROBLEM

"Boys, you're all wet," said Mom as they entered the kitchen. "Dundee, I should still be angry with you, but I can't stay mad at you forever." Her voice softened. "After all, you are my favorite doggie." She began to wipe off his paws with an old towel. "And as for you, Tyler, quick get out of that wet jacket and put on something dry."

When Dundee returned in a cozy sweater, Mom said, "I've got some cheese and crackers for you."

He could barely eat the cheese cube, although it was tasty. Dundee slipped a cracker to Tyler who just let it fall to the floor. Mom noticed their sad faces.

"You both look like you have something heavy on your hearts." She leaned over the pooch. "Dundee, I forgive you for being such a wild thing today. You know I love you." Tyler looked up with sad doggie eyes, his ears bent low.

Then Mom took Dundee by the hand and led him to the couch in the den. She fluffed one of the pillows and pulled

Dundee onto the couch near her. She put her arm around his shoulder and snuggled closer. "What's wrong, son? Did you have a rough day at school?" She gently brushed the hair off his face and waited a moment. "You look so sad." Dundee turned to her shoulder and began to sob.

Tyler, who had been sitting at her feet, jumped onto the couch and put his head in Mom's lap and joined in mournfully. The mother just sat there confused.

Dundee wiped his nose with the top of his hand and began to sob. "Mom, did you ever wish for something that came true and then realized it wasn't what you wanted after all?"

Mom thought for a minute and then replied, "Yes, I remember how much I wanted a piano when I was a little girl. When Grandma and Gramps bought me one and made me practice every day, I wished I had asked for a baseball glove instead."

Dundee grinned and Tyler raised his head to listen.

"Another time I wished for a baby sister. But, Grandma and Gramps brought home a baby brother. I was surprised, and disappointed. Seemed all they did was fuss over him. People came over and said how cute he was. Boy, was I jealous, thinking they loved him more than they loved me."

"Really?" asked Dundee.

"Yes, really. Eventually, I figured they loved us both the same. Just that some days they loved one of us more than the other. It all evens out."

Dundee chuckled.

"You know," she continued. "It took me years to understand that. Eventually, Uncle Jack taught me how to catch a baseball. And I can still play Christmas carols on the piano." She smiled. "Things do work out, most of the time."

Tyler and Dundee looked at each other thinking *Oh, great. Does this mean we have to get used to this?"*

Dundee leaned over to pet Tyler and whispered, "Oh no. I don't want to be a boy forever."

Tyler started a low growl, shaking his head side to side. *Great, just great. I'm not the doggie type either.*

Instinctively, Mom felt her son's head, thinking he surely must be ill. There was no fever, only a miserable little boy and an equally unhappy dog.

Neither creature felt like eating much that night. Both went up to bed early. Mom made some tea and read a story to her darlings in bed. Dundee looked onto the pages as Tyler huddled in a ball nearby.

The wind picked up and blew the curtains at the window. It had stopped raining but they could see lightening in the distance. The sky had a tinge of green. There was a funny smell, like chlorine bleach that Mom used to clean the bathroom.

"Mom, this is weird," said Dundee. "I'm scared."

"No need, son. The funny smell is ozone. It happens sometimes during a lightning storm. But in the morning, everything will smell fresh. I promise."

Dundee settled down and they finished the story.

Mom went over to close the window, but left it cracked, just a little as she said, "Tomorrow we're going to move your bed to the other side of the room. I don't like it so close to the window."

"Why, Mom?"

"I was reading that scientists are researching something strange that happens when a person makes a wish around ozone."

"You mean it makes wishes come true?"

"Not sure. But it's probably best not to get too close to that funny smell. Just in case," she replied. "You know what Grandma always says, 'Be careful what you wish for.'"

Tyler and Dundee looked at each other again thinking, *Hmmmmm....*

She tucked Dundee under the covers and patted Tyler's head. Then she kissed both her "boys," Dundee on his forehead and Tyler on his snout. Turning out the lights, she tiptoed out of the room.

After Mom's footsteps faded in the hallway, Dundee and Tyler went to the window. The sky was a pale green and the aroma was greater than before. They sat on the bed facing each other and inhaled a deep breath, making a wish just as the raindrops started splashing against the glass.

The two friends climbed back into bed and held each other close. Both were of the same mind.

"I just don't think I can go to school tomorrow and pretend to be you," said Dundee. "It's too hard."

Tyler whined, *What if I have to spend the rest of my life on all fours looking up people's noses and sniffing dog butts?"*

Dundee laughed. "It's really not so bad, but we'll figure it out tomorrow, buddy," said Dundee. "After all, we're both pretty smart, right?" Dundee rolled on his side and slipped his arm over his friend's warm body.

Tyler nodded his head before getting comfortable. But he wasn't so sure anymore. The pitter patter of the rain sounded peaceful and he drifted off to sweeter dreams.

Chapter 12

THE WONDER OF SCIENCE

"Tyler, wake up," whispered Mom gently as she shook his shoulder. She felt his forehead but there was no fever. "Wake up, sleepyhead. It's a brand new day. The sun is shining finally, and the coach has already called for practice after school."

Tyler rubbed his eyes and looked into Mom's smiling face as she leaned over the bed.

"Let's go." She turned and gave Dundee a long pat from his head all the way to his tail. "That goes for you, too, Dundee."

Dundee yawned and stretched all four paws.

"Bet you're starving. How about some pancakes for breakfast?" She didn't bother to wait for an answer. She was already half way down the hall.

"Yeah, sure Mom," said Tyler waking from a dream. Slowly he got out of bed and walked to the bathroom, on two legs! He looked down and then at the familiar reflection in the hallway mirror. "It's me. It's really me. Yippee!"

Dundee followed him and jumped up in his familiar 'wanna dance' pose. The two of them jumped around the bathroom holding 'hands' as Tyler yelled "Wahoo!"

"What happened, Dundee?" Tyler looked at his face in the bathroom mirror. "Maybe it was the…what did Mom call it? Ozone? Who cares? Isn't it great?"

"Hey, I guess you're feeling better up there. Your breakfast is ready," called Mom.

"I'll be right down, Mom." Tyler went to the bathroom with his two feet on the ground, then splashed water onto his face and into his hair. He jumped into his clothes and brushed his teeth. As Tyler bounced down the stairs with a new spring in his step, Dundee ran ahead with a big doggie grin on his face.

Tyler poured himself some orange juice.

"I'm so glad you two are better," Mom said. She cracked the door so Dundee could come back in after doing his 'business' outside. "I was getting worried about you, my two favorite boys in the whole world."

Tyler inhaled his pancakes smothered with warm maple syrup saving a piece for Dundee. Then the boy gulped a whole glass of milk.

Mom looked aghast. "Where are your manners, son? You ate your breakfast as if you were a dog," said Mom.

"Oh, Mom, this is delicious. So much better than dog food." He put his hand to his mouth hoping that Mom didn't hear that comment.

"Dog food, you say?"

"I mean, that's why I always give Dundee a bite," Tyler said with a sly smile as he gave the last bite to Dundee. When Mom took his plate to the sink, Tyler wiped his brow, looked at Dundee and said, "Whew."

Dundee didn't notice. He was too busy licking the syrup from his chops.

Tyler slung his book bag over his shoulder and headed out the door with Dundee at his heels. "See you after school, Mom. Thanks for the great breakfast, really great." Then turning to his furry friend, he said, "Let's go, buddy." The two of them met Kevin walking to the bus stop.

"Tyler, that was some storm last night, huh?" Kevin said as he paused to give Dundee a pat.

"Yup, like nothing I ever experienced before."

"Me, neither," said Kevin.

I bet not, thought Dundee as the three of them continued toward the other children waiting on the corner.

In a few minutes the familiar roar came around the corner. Tyler gave Dundee an extra big hug and said, "See you after school, pal."

Dundee gave Tyler an extra wet kiss and sat silently as the school bus went around the bend. Then he went running home for a delicious doggie biscuit with his tail wagging as if to say "All's well."

At school, the boys raced to Mrs. Duncan's room, as usual. During the Pledge of Allegiance, Tyler scanned the finger painting masterpieces that were dried and displayed. While the other children were sharpening their pencils, he walked around the classroom to look for Dundee's. It was swirls of blues and greens with a big yellow sun at the top. *Not bad for a dog.* It made him smile with pride.

After seeing Tyler act so strange yesterday, Alfred decided not to mess with Tyler's things after all. Jessica didn't come near him all day. On the math quiz, Tyler did OK, although he didn't study.

During DEAR Time, Mrs. Duncan surprised the class with a baseball story about Jackie Robinson. By the end of the school day, the sun dried all the puddles making it a perfect afternoon for baseball practice.

On the way home, Kevin said, "I sure hope you can catch the ball today better than yesterday. The rain made you a lousy fielder."

"Sometimes, thunderstorms do strange things. But today, with the sun out, I can catch any fly ball about as well as Dundee," Tyler replied.

Sure enough, Tyler did great at practice. Dundee enjoyed it too, since all the kids gave him a loving pat. Some shared their popcorn with him or a piece of hot-dog. He even got to lick an ice cream cone that one of the kids dropped on the ground.

What a great day to be a dog, thought Dundee.

"What a great day to be a kid," said Tyler looking up at a cloudless blue sky, a perfect day.

That night the two buddies snuggled close and wondered if yesterday had been only a dream. Not taking any chances, Tyler got up and closed the window all the way.

Getting into bed and getting comfy under the covers he said, "Hey, Mom, about rearranging my room..." before drifting off into a world of Little League home runs.

Dundee dreamed too, about surprising Mrs. Duncan with that pesky squirrel.

The End.

I hope you have enjoyed reading MY DOG, ME. Here are some thoughts to share:

1. Have you ever wanted to be another animal for a day? Which kind? Why?

2. What would you do if you got stuck in the body of an animal?

3. If you have a brother or sister, what kind of animal does he or she remind you of? Why? How about Mom? Dad?

4. If you could have a wish come true, what would it be? Why?

5. What does the world look like through the eyes of a bird? A snake? A dolphin?

6. Ask an adult to share a story of a favorite pet he had as a child.

73317962R00043

Made in the USA
Columbia, SC
04 September 2019